Adoption is admirable. Sometimes the journey can be very hard.
For all the forever-families who choose love every day, this one is for you.

For Dibora – you are a bright and shining star; use your light for goodness.
All my love, Mom

This book belongs to
Boodles' Buddy:

_____

_____

_____

Published by

Purposeful Goods, LLC
99 Almaden Boulevard, Suite 500
San Jose, California 95113
purposefulgoods.com

Copyright ©2015 by Purposeful Goods, LLC
All rights reserved.
No part of this publication may be reproduced
in any form without written permission
from the publisher.

This product conforms to CPSIA 2008.

Printed in the United States of America.

Being adopted is super-duper special!

Created by Christine Burger

Purposeful Goods™

Hi! My name is Boodles and I'm your Buddy!

You are growing up and getting bigger and bigger every day.

Becoming a "big kid" is super-duper fun. I call it being a "Biggie."

A lot of new and exciting things are going to happen in your life. You will have lots of questions and there will be many things you will want to know about.
I'm here to be your Buddy and help explain them to you!

Do you know what "being adopted" means?

It takes a man and a woman to make a baby. Babies grow inside their birth-mommies' tummies until they are big enough to be born.

Many babies stay with the woman whose tummy they came from—their birth-mommy. Some very special babies do not. They get adopted by their forever-families.

Forever-mommies and forever-daddies have lots of love in their hearts.
They want to share their love with a super-duper special boy or girl.

You are very, very special. I'm so glad I get to be your Buddy!

Birth-mommies love the babies that come out of their tummies, but sometimes they cannot take care of them.

They love their babies so much that they let them be adopted by a forever-family who will love them and take good care of them forever.

There are lots of reasons why a birth-mommy may not be able to take care of a baby.

We can ask your forever-mommy and daddy your adoption story.

Sometimes a forever-mommy cannot have a baby in her tummy and sometimes a forever-mommy can, but wants more children to love.

Forever-mommies and daddies choose to find a little child who needs to be adopted.

They want that special girl or boy more than anything in the whole wide world.

When forever-mommies and daddies get the news that their forever-child is coming, it is a super-duper happy time!

Sometimes forever-daddies and mommies have to wait a long time for their forever-child. But, that's okay because when the right time comes, their forever-child arrives!

Sometimes their forever-child is from far, far away in a different country; sometimes they are close by.

Now that you are a Biggie, your forever-daddy and mommy can tell you what continent and country you came from. Since I'm your Buddy, you can tell me all about it!

Sometimes forever-children look just like their forever-mommies and daddies; sometimes they look different. You may not have the same color skin or eyes or hair. But guess what—your forever-family thinks you are perfect just the way you are. I think you're amazing too!

As you grow bigger, you will notice that you may be just like your forever-mommy and daddy in many ways.

Maybe you will smile just like your mommy. Or, maybe you will laugh just like your daddy.

You might like to go swimming like your mommy or eat ice cream just like your daddy. Can you think of how you are just like your forever-mommy and daddy? I think that's super-duper neat!

A forever-daddy and mommy always take care of their forever-child. This means that you will always have warm clothes, yummy food and fun toys. You will have a soft bed to sleep in and a home to share with your family.

Having a forever-family means that you are safe and you are loved forever.

 Because "everybody needs a buddy sometimes," Christine Burger created *Your Buddy Boodles*. Boodles' motto, "I will wipe away your tears, chase away your fears and be there with good cheer." Teachable moments, tender explanations and embracing "the why," makes Boodles a parent's buddy too.

Founder of celebrated children's skin care brand Noodle & Boo, Christine has embraced her roles as a mom and an entrepreneur by continuing to find ways to use her personal experiences to create products for parents who also want the very best for their children. She truly believes, "There is nothing more wonderful or more important than caring for and loving a child."
Boodles would agree.